For Edith Gordon – E.M.
For Wazza, and thanks for all the fish – P.H.

About the story

This is the European version of a traditional Chinese Mandarin story known as *The Seed*.
It was retold by Charlotte Demi Hunt Huang as *The Empty Pot* (Henry Holt & Company, 1990).
The author heard it from Amy Douglas, who heard it from Shonaleigh, who heard it from Taffy Thomas...

The King and the Seed copyright © Frances Lincoln Limited 2009
Text copyright © Eric Maddern 2009
Illustrations copyright © Paul Hess 2009

First published in Great Britain and the USA in 2009 by
Frances Lincoln Children's Books, 4 Torriano Mews,
Torriano Avenue, London NW5 2RZ
www.franceslincoln.com

British Library Cataloguing in Publication Data available on request

ISBN: 978-1-84507-926-0

Illustrated with watercolours and coloured pencil

Set in Berkeley

Printed in Singapore

1 3 5 7 9 8 6 4 2

The King and the Seed

Eric Maddern

Illustrated by Paul Hess

F

FRANCES LINCOLN
CHILDREN'S BOOKS

King Karnak was worried. He looked in the mirror
one morning and saw an old man staring back at him,
his hair silver, his eyes cornered with crow's feet.
No doubt about it: he didn't have long for this world.

He had another worry too. He and his wife had
never been blessed with children. Now, sadly, the
Queen had died and the King had no heir. It was
causing him sleepless nights.

So he had a good long think, and finally came up
with an idea.

The King sent out a proclamation: "Let anyone who wants to be king after me come to the palace and take part in a competition."

A wave of excitement rippled through the land. The knights and nobles thought they were in with a chance. The competition was bound to be a tournament. They would fight each other in single combat on horseback with lances and swords. Whoever was the best fighter would be the next king – it was as simple as that. Or so they thought.

So they set about sharpening their swords, polishing their armour and doing their press-ups, practising hard for the big day.

On the day of the competition, hundreds of lords and nobles splendidly arrayed in armour and riding handsome horses gathered outside the castle. Their weapons glinted in the sun. They bustled about, jostling and talking in loud voices, each trying to look more kingly than the next.

But there was one in the colourful crowd who wasn't a lord or a noble, who didn't have a horse or armour. This was Jack, a farmer's son, who lived near the castle. He hadn't come to be king, but just because he loved excitement and wanted to see what would happen.

Suddenly the King's Crier ordered everyone to leave their horses and weapons outside and enter the castle courtyard. A great grumbling arose from the nobles, who felt cheated of their tournament. They traipsed into the castle, muttering and complaining to each other.

Then the buglers trumpeted a fanfare and everyone fell silent. A great oak door swung open and the King stepped out.

The Crier shouted: "Form an orderly queue!"

Orderly queue? The knights and nobles didn't form orderly queues. They pushed and shoved people around. But this was the King and they had to do what he said. So they huffed and puffed and shuffled about, forming a ragged line.

Then the King pulled a pouch from his cloak and took out something small. It was a seed.

"I'm going to give you each one of these," he said. "Take it away and see what you can grow. Come back in six months and from what you've grown, I'll decide who will be king after me."

There was a rumble of protest. Grow a seed? Pah! That was peasants' work! These knights wanted a proper manly fight. They didn't want to grow seeds. Still, if it meant they could be the next king, they would have to do it. So, one by one, they grudgingly took a seed from the King.

Jack was watching this with amusement. Being a farmer's boy, he knew all about growing seeds. So he joined the line and got his very own seed.

Back home, Jack found a little pot. He filled it with compost, pressed in the seed and watered it. He knew some seeds like the dark, so he put it in a warm cupboard. Each day he checked for a telltale little green sprout, but nothing came up.

So he put it on a window ledge in the sunshine. He watched and watered it every day, but still nothing grew. Then he stopped watering for a while, but it made no difference.

"It needs stronger manure," Jack thought. So he scraped up some rooster poo from the chicken shed. That would do the trick. But a week later there was no green shoot to be seen.

Two months passed, and still Jack's seed hadn't sprouted. He'd tried everything, even talking and singing to his little pot. By now he was desperate. So he climbed on to the roof and put the pot next to the chimney. "Warm and sunny here," he thought. But still nothing grew.

Finally he took his pot to the forest, thinking the seed might like trees all around. But it made not the slightest difference.

At last, after three months, Jack gave up. "I'll never make this seed grow now."

When the day for showing the plants came, Jack wasn't planning to go. But his family said he'd tried hard and that he should go, just to see how it turned out. So he did. And tucked under his coat was his little pot, with the seed he'd loved so much.

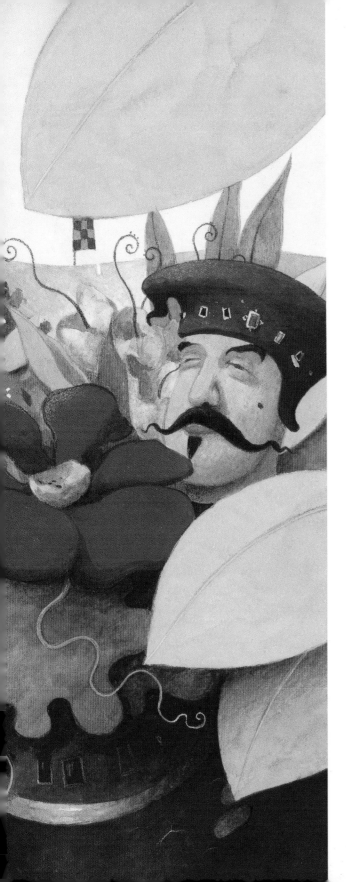

Outside the castle the lords were preening like peacocks, eager to show off the blooms and blossoms they'd grown from the King's seed. There were roses, poppies and hollyhocks; dahlias, azaleas and pansies; lilies, marigolds, foxgloves; sunflowers and chrysanthemums. It looked and smelled like a garden centre in June.

When the trumpet sounded, the lords bustled into the courtyard, proudly displaying their beautiful plants. This time they didn't have to be asked to line up.

And there, skulking in the shadows, was Jack, his little pot of nothing-but-compost tucked under his coat.

The King walked on to the podium and the crowd hushed.

The first lord stepped forward and presented his wondrous flower. The King examined it briefly and said: "Yes, very good, thank you. Next!"

The second lord stepped up and received the same response: "Yes, very good, thank you. Next!"

And so it went on. To everyone who came up, the King said the same words: "Yes, very good, thank you. Next!"

Jack was not going to go up, for he had nothing to show. But suddenly, when the line had dwindled almost to nothing, someone pushed him forward and he found himself before the King.

"I'm sorry, Your Majesty," Jack spluttered. "I couldn't grow that seed you gave me. I tried everything."

He began to move away from the King's strong gaze, but a royal hand clapped him on the shoulder.

"What's your name, boy?"

"Jack, my lord."

"Jack," said the King. "You have done well!"

"'Well, my lord?" said Jack. "But I grew nothing from that seed, sire."

"Jack," chuckled the King, "I don't know where those knights got their wonderful flowers from, but they weren't from the seeds I gave them. You see, I boiled those seeds for a whole hour before giving them out. Not one of them should have sprouted."

Jack's head started to spin.

"Jack," continued the King, "Of all these contenders, you were the only one with the courage and honesty to tell me the truth. And courage and honesty are what I'm looking for in the person who will be king after me. And so, Jack, I declare *you* my heir and successor!"

Jack was stunned. You could have knocked him down with a flower. And, to tell the truth, he wasn't sure he wanted to be king.

Luckily the old King lived a few years more, giving Jack time to get used to the idea – and to learn some kingly arts, such as how to ride a horse and speak in a loud voice.

Finally, when the old King died, Jack was crowned in his place: King Jack the First, King Jack the Only!

King Jack was not just brave and honest. He loved Nature too. He loved seeing things grow. So soon, flowers and forests were springing up everywhere. Nature came into cities. People went out into Nature. Many of the lords even hung up their swords and picked up garden forks instead.

Best of all, when King Jack saw how much his people loved growing things, he set up a Royal Flower Show, a kind of flower tournament, for everyone to display what they grew.

And so it has continued, from that day to this.